Poetry for Young People
Animal Poems

Edited by John Hollander

Illustrations by Simona Mulazzani

STERLING

New York / London

www.sterlingpublishing.com/kids

For Adam and Lucy and Noah,
once again
　　　　　　　　　—John Hollander

A Daniele e Margherita
　　　　　　　　—Simona Mulazzani

Library of Congress Cataloging-in-Publication Data

Poetry for young people : animal poems / edited by John Hollander ; illustrations by
Simona Mulazzani.
　　　p. cm.
　　Includes index.
　　ISBN 1-4027-0926-9
　　1. Animals—Juvenile poetry. I. Hollander, John. II. Mulazzani, Simona.
PN6110.A7P64 2004
808.81'9362–dc22　　　　　　　　　　　　　　　　　　　　　　　2004013314

The haiku—"The Rats," "The Crow and the Fox," and "The Animals Rest"—were
translated by John Hollander. "The Sloth," copyright 1950 by Theodore Roethke, from
Collected Poems of Theodore Roethke by Theodore Roethke. Used by permission of Doubleday,
a division of Random House, Inc. "Little Fish" by D. H. Lawrence, from *The Complete Poems
of D. H. Lawrence* by D. H. Lawrence, edited by V. de Sola Pinto & F. W. Roberts, copyright
© 1964, 1971 by Angelo Ravagli and C. M. Weekley, Executors of the Estate of Frieda
Lawrence Ravagli. Used by permission of Viking Penguin, a division of Penguin Group
(USA) Inc. "Bison Crossing Near Mt. Rushmore" by May Swenson. Used with permission
of the Literary Estate of May Swenson. Published in *Things Taking Place* by May Swenson,
1978. "Riding a Nervous Horse" by Vickie Hearne. From *Nervous Horses* © 1980.
Used by permission of the University of Texas Press.

6　7　8　9　10　11　12　13　14　15　16　17　18　19　20

Published by Sterling Publishing Co., Inc.
387 Park Avenue South, New York, NY 10016
Text © 2004 by John Hollander
Illustrations © 2004 by Simona Mulazzani
Distributed in Canada by Sterling Publishing
c/o Canadian Manda Group, 165 Dufferin Street
Toronto, Ontario, Canada M6K 3H6
Distributed in Australia by Capricorn Link (Australia) Pty. Ltd.
P.O. Box 704, Windsor, NSW 2756, Australia

Manufactured in China 12/09
All rights reserved
Sterling ISBN-13: 978-1-4027-0926-5
Sterling ISBN-10: 1-4027-0926-9

For information about custom editions, special sales, premium and
corporate purchases, please contact Sterling Special Sales
Department at 800-805-5489 or specialsales@sterlingpub.com

CONTENTS

INTRODUCTION

This is a book of poetry about animals. And in a less obvious way, the poems in it are all about people as well. Written across four centuries, in North America, Europe, and East Asia, each of them records a particular sort of contact between a human being and either a kind of animal or a particular creature of that kind. And part of what makes each contact different is the particular point of view of each poem, the way in which it regards the animal in question.

People have always lived with, and among, all sorts of animals—creatures large and small, of the ground, of water, of trees, and of the air. In primitive times, certain animals were only killed for food or clothing. Later in human history, they were also kept alive and taken care of, to provide milk or eggs or wool, for example, or used for help in work or simply loved as companions. Some of the earliest art we have—cave paintings from southern Europe—consists of beautifully drawn animals. Carved or modeled images of animals representing particular pagan gods and goddesses were the objects of worship long ago. And early in the book of Genesis in the Bible, we read how Adam gave names "to the fowl of the air and to every beast of the field" (as the King James Version translates it). Naming the animals (and, of course, noticing things about them) was the very first human activity in the garden of Eden. It thus can seem that a human obligation to take animals very seriously was there in us all from the very beginning.

Certainly, poets—particularly from the later eighteenth century on—have responded to that obligation. Homer, the earliest of Western poets, tells in great detail in his *Odyssey* of how its hero Odysseus, returning to his home in disguise after many years, is recognized by his dog, Argos. In early times generally, particular animals were considered to be symbols as well as natural creatures: The dog was associated with faithfulness, fidelity; the owl with wisdom; the donkey with humility. The lion and the eagle were thought of as kings of the land and the air. All of these associations produced many references to animals in poetry of many kinds.

Natural history—as the earliest forms of zoology, botany, and geology used to be called—goes back to ancient Greek times. The earliest written accounts and descriptions of animals and their lives are an interesting mixture of good observation and well-known fictions. Until modern times, people knew more about domestic animals than about wild ones. Domestic animals could be both those of the household (pet dogs, cats, and birds) and those kept for work or food (horses, donkeys, cows, sheep, fowl, etc.) It was only with modern zoos, the study of natural history at all levels of schooling, and most recently, wonderful filming of even the most obscure and rare creatures, that actual knowledge about their lives and habits replaced poetic folklore.

There is a lot of fine poetry, both older and modern, about purely mythical or fabulous animals. Among these were the Unicorn, about which the great German poet Rainer Maria Rilke wrote a sonnet beginning "This is the animal that doesn't exist." The poem goes on to say that people loved the idea of it so much that "a pure creature came into being." Then there was the Chimera—part serpent, part lion, part eagle—who was killed by the hero Bellerophon riding another mythical beast, the horse with wings named Pegasus. The Phoenix was an imaginary bird. Only one of them existed at a time. Every 500 years, it burned up in flames and then rose again from its own ashes, "her birthplace when self-born again!," in the words of the early nineteenth-century English poet George Darley. A famous mythical creature was imagined in the late 1890s by the American comic writer Gelett Burgess, who wrote

> I never saw a Purple Cow,
> I never hope to see one,
> But I can tell you anyhow,
> I'd rather see than be one!

But the poems in this collection all concern real, natural animals, whether common or rare, great or small, wild or tame, encountered in everyday life and in zoos, or only read of in books or seen in photographic images. (Before photography, of course, drawings or paintings could show actual or mythical creatures alike.) Each of them is about some bird or mammal or reptile or insect or sea creature. Each poem here is addressed to, or spoken by, or describes, or tells a story of an encounter with the animal in question. And yet, there is a strange way in which poems can make a real animal just a bit mythical or imaginary. They can give some bird or beast or fish a particular meaning it never had. The Oven Bird in Robert Frost's sonnet might have led a poet to write about what it means to build a nest close to the ground, which this bird indeed does. But Frost focuses on the matter of when during the year its singing is heard, and what that might mean. His oven bird seems to become a kind of philosophy teacher, raising an important unanswered question (the way good teachers often do) at the end of the poem.

A poem can deliberately think about an animal in a way different from some popular view of it. The chameleon, for example, is a kind of lizard that changes color depending on his background at the moment. Chameleons back in Shakespeare's time were said to have fed themselves on air. And people who dishonestly presented themselves differently to various others were called "chameleons." Marianne Moore knew all that when she wrote her "To a Chameleon," but she concentrated on the powerful beauty of the animal's various hues. Then she went on to change the old fable of living on air to one about eating all the colors. And the fact that spiders spin webs in order to trap flying insects for food does not interest Walt Whitman when he contemplates the creature in his poem "A Noiseless, Patient Spider." Rather, its work represents for him a way that his own soul can to reach out and across space to other people: the way, indeed, a poet's language does.

Poems can also speak for creatures who cannot speak for themselves. That is, the "I" of a poem can be an animal as easily as it can be a sort of person. There is the kind of creature that in the tradition of Aesop's fables "personifies" a particular human characteristic, like Emerson's squirrel getting the better of a huge mountain, or La Fontaine's wily and flattering fox tricking the vain crow. Perhaps animal fables started out as a way of hiding harsh criticism of actual people by talking of their faults as being those of animals: this was said of the Greek slave Aesop, who was supposed to have invented such fables. They can also be imagined to have natures of their own, like Kipling's wolves singing the hunting song of their pack, sounding something like a human hunter, or the owl and cat, Edward Lear's courting couple, or the ladybird, called "clock-a-clay," of John Clare's poem, giving wonderfully clear and detailed descriptions of the natural world it lives in. Christina Rossetti's animals, however, remain unable to speak; the title of her "Words for the Dumb" might mean "words for dumb animals to say," but the poet means something else. Her title phrase has the sense of "words spoken in behalf of animals who can't speak them," and those words are directed *to* humans: "Pity the sorrows of a poor old Dog / Who wags his tail a-begging in his need . . . / Spare Puss who trusts us purring on our hearth . . . " Humans have language with which to plead for themselves. Animals don't, and only humans can do it for them.

There are many different ways in which the speakers in poems address various animals. Sometimes we are made to feel almost as if the animal could reply in the same language (but the poem doesn't let us hear this). An example would be the squirrel questioned by William Butler Yeats, who doesn't even reply, as Frost's bird does, "in all but words." Most often, the

6

poem's speaking voice seems to acknowledge that it's talking to the animal as a particular way of talking to itself and/or to other human listeners. Leigh Hunt, addressing the grasshopper and the cricket, speaks this way. And when Yeats, in another poem, questions the animal in "The Cat and the Moon," he sounds as if he's still talking to the reader, as he has been all along. The most extreme case of this may be the speaker of William Blake's poem addressing the tiger. To a careful reader, he seems to be calling out to a creature he has imagined, speaking to himself while a real tiger stands by quite ignoring him. In many other cases, too, poets' talking to animals is a way of talking to themselves. This is something all of us who have pets or even live with farm animals do, of course (even though our dogs seem to listen to us talking to them while our cats do not). And we don't get angry or annoyed when animals don't answer us—often, silently, we do their answering for them. This happens a lot in poems about animals. But poets will ask questions and raise issues that some of us might wonder about silently, but never ask aloud, when thinking of an animal. In William Wordsworth's "To a Butterfly," the poet wants the butterfly to remain nearby because of the "converse" or conversation they have, but the butterfly's part in this is to evoke memories in the poet's mind, rather than to tell stories in an imaginary language of its own. (And how different, in any case, this creature is from the butterflies in Moritake's haiku, which are at first mistaken for petals of fallen blossoms flying back up to their tree branches. These are not so much individual insects as bits of color, shape, and motion, startling to see because of that mistake.)

A poem can notice things about creatures of different kinds, and about the way they behave. Poetry can be very careful in its observation, and yet report in strange ways on what has been seen. Nobody would think that a small snake looks like a comb, but Emily Dickinson's wonderful lines from the poem beginning "A narrow fellow in the grass"

> The grass divides as with a comb,
> A spotted shaft is seen;
> And then it closes at your feet
> And opens further on

suggests that its way of moving low in the grass makes the grass look as if it were being combed.

Poets will often think about an animal in the light of a good deal of knowledge, whether of some particular facts learned from the study of zoology or from human history. May Swenson's poem "Bison Crossing near Mount Rushmore" about a herd of bison seen near a famous national monument by a herd of tourists comes out of knowledge of how the buffaloes behave in a group while moving. And it is full of an unstated awareness of how human civilization, moving westward across North America, drove them almost (until very recently) to the point of extinction. And the poet and animal trainer Vicki Hearne, in "Riding a Nervous Horse," writes out of a wide and deep acquaintance with horses and their ways, and yet her poem is nothing like a textbook or instruction manual.

The poems in this collection are of quite different sorts. They talk or sing or tell short tales or describe or imagine—and from many points of view. Some, for example, like Walt Whitman's verses on the spider or John Clare's on the ladybird can seem to look at very tiny creatures through an imaginary sort of microscope. Poetry celebrates animals in a wide of variety of ways. The more we all get to know and understand animals, the more new and interesting questions poets will continue to raise about them, and their likenesses to, and differences from, us.

THREE WITH WINGS

Something different is noted about each flying creature in these little poems. They are of the kind called "haiku" in Japanese, their three lines measured in syllables—five, then seven, then five. Unique to Japanese poetry until the twentieth century, haiku were written across the centuries, and still are today. Each poem takes only a moment to say, and each one is about a quick moment of attention to the bird's or butterfly's flight up or down and what they suggest. In the first, the speaker is puzzled by fallen summer leaves that seem to fly up and re-attach themselves, but then realizes what the rising petals actually are. In the second, the black crow alighting on a bare branch is both a sign of autumn and a picture of what autumn is like. The last is about a small skylark that sings from so high up that one can barely see it.

Arakida Moritake (sixteenth century)
Fallen flowers now
To their branch returning I
See—the butterflies!

Basho (seventeenth century)
On a dry dead branch
A crow has been settling down . . .
Nightfall in autumn.

Ampu (late eighteenth century)
Nothing but a song
Descending, and after that
No skylark is there.

THE TYGER
William Blake (1757–1827)

William Blake was a great visionary poet and artist who made up and illustrated long and mysterious poems explaining how the world got to be what it's like. Some of his short pieces are more complicated than they seem. This famous poem is composed of questions that are not given answers. It is often taken to be an expression of awe, and a celebration of some kind of mighty creative power as seen in the tiger (Blake spelled it in the older way). But we must remember that the speaker, the person addressing the tiger, is not the poet himself. He is a fictional character the poet has invented, and he seems increasingly terrified as he makes his strange queries. (Blake's own illustration for this poem shows the tiger looking as gentle as a household cat.) Finally, in the repetition of the first stanza at the very end, notice how "could frame" has become "dare frame."

Tyger! Tyger! burning bright
In the forests of the night,
What immortal hand or eye
Could frame thy fearful symmetry?

In what distant deeps or skies
Burnt the fire of thine eyes?
On what wings dare he aspire?
What the hand dare seize the fire?

And what shoulder, and what art,
Could twist the sinews of thy heart,
And when thy heart began to beat,
What dread hand? and what dread feet?

frame—*build*
symmetry —*beautifully ordered, balanced arrangement*
aspire—*rise upward*
On what wings?—*refers to the Greek myth of Icarus, who flew too close to the sun on the wax wings his father had made, and fell into the sea.*
What the hand dare seize the fire?—*Prometheus, in Greek mythology, stole fire from the gods to give to mankind, and was punished for it.*
sinews—*muscles*

What the hammer? what the chain?
In what furnace was thy brain?
What the anvil? what dread grasp
Dare its deadly terrors clasp?

When the stars threw down their spears,
And water'd heaven with their tears,
Did he smile his work to see?
Did he who made the Lamb make thee?

Tyger! Tyger! burning bright
In the forests of the night,
What immortal hand or eye,
Dare frame thy fearful symmetry?

anvil—*curved metal block on which hot iron is shaped by beating*
stars—*the angels who rebelled against God and were thrown out*
of heaven in John Milton's great epic,"Paradise Lost"

11

THE ELEPHANT
Hilaire Belloc (1870–1953)

Hilaire (pronounced "Hillary") Belloc was a British writer who composed, among other things, some sharply witty verses for children as well as for adults. This tiny poem is made up of only a single quatrain (rhymed stanza of four lines). Belloc's observation speaks of what adults and very small children often feel, on first seeing elephants or pictures of them—that they have two tails. Perhaps the grown-ups only wonder at the relative sizes of trunk and tail because they still hang onto some of this childhood impression without realizing it.

When people call this beast to mind,
   They marvel more and more
At such a little tail behind,
   So large a trunk before.

THE OVEN BIRD
Robert Frost (1874–1963)

Robert Frost was our great modern poet of New England country life, but his poems are all about broad human concerns. Here he considers a bird whose song is not an awakening one of spring, like those of so many other birds. Instead, he sings of the middle of summer, and of midpoints, generally. His call is more like saying and telling than singing, and his last question is one like "In the middle of it all, is the glass of summer half-full or half-empty?" Frost was probably also thinking of how the oven bird's call is usually said to sound like the words "Teacher! Teacher!" The bird in his poem certainly is one.

There is a singer everyone has heard,
Loud, a mid-summer and a mid-wood bird
Who makes the solid tree trunks sound again.
He says that leaves are old and that for flowers,
Mid-summer is to spring as one to ten.
He says the early petal-fall is past
When pear and cherry bloom went down in showers
On sunny days a moment overcast;
And comes that other fall we name the fall.
He says the highway dust is over all.
The bird would cease and be as other birds
But that he knows in singing not to sing.
The question that he frames in all   but words
Is what to make of a diminished thing.

Make of—both "make sense out of, understand" and "make up or construct something with"
diminished—made less

13

A NARROW FELLOW

Emily Dickinson (1830–1886)

This poem about a snake focuses on what it's like to see one (and almost always suddenly). The poem describes the snake in an amusing and rather pleasant way, but the last two lines are startling: the snake is harmless, and yet the speaker feels some kind of dread so deep that she calls it simply "zero at the bone." These last lines are as sudden and exciting as the appearance of the snake at the beginning. Emily Dickinson, one of our greatest poets, lived in Amherst, Massachusetts. She celebrated her minute private observations and perceptions in hundreds of remarkably original poems.

A narrow fellow in the grass
Occasionally rides;
You may have met him,—did you not?
His notice sudden is.

The grass divides as with a comb,
A spotted shaft is seen;
And then it closes at your feet
And opens further on.

He likes a boggy acre,
A floor too cool for corn.
Yet when a child, and barefoot,
I more than once at morn,

Have passed, I thought, a whip-lash
Unbraiding in the sun,—
When, stooping to secure it,
It wrinkled, and was gone.

Several of nature's people
I know, and they know me;
I feel for them a transport
Of cordiality;

But never met this fellow,
Attended, or alone,
Without a tighter breathing,
And zero at the bone.

notice—*announcement of his presence*
boggy—*marshy*
transport—*strong feeling of joy*
attended—*accompanied*

14

TO A CHAMELEON

Marianne Moore (1887–1972)

Marianne Moore, one of the finest poets of the twentieth century, lived in Brooklyn, N.Y. She wrote of animals, both real and mythical, in a variety of ways. In these poems, she considers two small animals, both of which have "a fluctuating charm" in their changeable colors. The chameleon, a tropical lizard, changes color back and forth, snapping up rainbow colors "for food," as if they were the insects it does indeed live on. The transparent jellyfish—which will sting you if you touch it—seems to radiate yellowish (amber) and purple (amethyst) from its reflective surface.

Hid by the august foliage and fruit of the grape vine,
Twine
   Your anatomy
     Round the pruned and polished stem,
      Chameleon.
      Fire laid upon
     An emerald as long as
   The Dark King's massy
One,
Could not snap the spectrum up for food as you have done.

Chameleon—*tropical lizard that changes color back and forth*
twine—*twist*
massy—*heavy and dense*
spectrum—*the range of colors, as in a rainbow*

A JELLY-FISH

Visible, invisible,
   a fluctuating charm
an amber-tinctured amethyst
   inhabits it, your arm
approaches and it opens
   and it closes; you had meant
to catch it and it quivers;
   you abandon your intent …

fluctuating—*changing back and forth*
amethyst—*purplish gemstone*

THE SLOTH
Theodore Roethke (1908–1963)

Theodore Roethke, an important poet from Michigan, wrote much of his best work while teaching at the University of Washington in Seattle. These amusing observations on the mammal who hangs upside down from tree branches was one of a number of poems he wrote for children. The word "sloth" comes from the early English "slowth," so you can see that the creature was aptly named. Roethke's poem is playful in its view of the sloth, but takes something about him very seriously as well.

In moving-slow he has no Peer.
You ask him something in his Ear,
He thinks about it for a Year;

And then, before he says a Word
There, upside-down (unlike a Bird),
He will assume that you have Heard—

A most Ex-as-per-at-ing Lug.
But should you call his manner Smug,
He'll sigh and give his Branch a Hug;

Then off again to Sleep he goes,
Still swaying gently by his Toes,
And you just *know* he knows he knows.

peer—*equal*
smug—*blindly convinced of one's own rightness*
lug—*clumsy fool*

16

FABLE

Ralph Waldo Emerson (1803–1882)

Animal fables have been associated for over 2,000 years with the name of Aesop, an ancient Greek writer (who may not have actually existed). In those stories, animals not only talk, but plan and believe, hope and promise, lie and sulk, and so forth—just like humans. Some fables have morals at the end—statements about what is and, particularly, what ought to be. Emerson was most famous as a philosophical essayist, but his poetry is very fine indeed. This fable is more interesting than if it were just about an underdog (the very small squirrel) outwitting a large adversary. Actually, the squirrel is saying that neither is "better," but that each is capable of important things.

The mountain and the squirrel
Had a quarrel;
And the former called the latter "Little Prig."
Bun replied,
"You are doubtless very big;
But all sorts of things and weather
Must be taken in together,
To make up a year
And a sphere.
And I think it no disgrace
To occupy my place.
If I'm not so large as you,
You are not so small as I,
And not half so spry.
I'll not deny you make
A very pretty squirrel track;
Talents differ; all is well and wisely put;
If I cannot carry forests on my back,
Neither can you crack a nut."

prig—*someone smug, narrow-minded*
bun—*squirrel, (as well as rabbit)*
sphere—*the planet Earth*
spry—*nimble, lively, active*

17

THE OWL AND THE PUSSY-CAT
Edward Lear (1812–1888)

Edward Lear was an English artist and writer of comical stories and poems, mostly for children, that he described as "nonsense." This is the most famous of his verses. Underneath its fabulous story lie two ways in which cats and some owls are indeed alike: they are both creatures who hunt at night, and the head of a horned owl, lit from behind, can look startlingly like a cat's head. And so perhaps their courtship and marriage here are somehow appropriate after all.

I

The Owl and the Pussy-Cat went to sea
   In a beautiful pea-green boat,
They took some honey, and plenty of money,
   Wrapped up in a five-pound note.
The Owl looked up to the stars above,
   And sang to a small guitar,
"O lovely Pussy, O Pussy, my love,
   What a beautiful Pussy you are,
      You are,
      You are!
What a beautiful Pussy you are!"

II

Pussy said to the Owl, "You elegant fowl!
   How charmingly sweet you sing!
O let us be married! too long we have tarried:
   But what shall we do for a ring?"
They sailed away, for a year and a day,
   To the land where the bong-tree grows;
And there in a wood a Piggy-wig stood
   With a ring at the end of his nose,
      His nose,
      His nose,
With a ring at the end of his nose.

III

"Dear Pig, are you willing to sell for one shilling
   Your ring?" Said the Piggy, "I will."
So they took it away, and were married next day
   By the Turkey who lives on the hill.
They dined on mince, and slices of quince,
   Which they ate with a runcible spoon;
And hand in hand, on the edge of the sand,
   They danced by the light of the moon,
     The moon,
     The moon,
They danced by the light of the moon.

five-pound note—*large-sized bill of paper money*
bong-tree—*nonsensical made-up tree*
runcible—*Lear's nonsense word for a spoon with one sharp*
   cutting edge

THE FROG AND THE MOUSE
Anonymous

This is one of many American versions of an English folk song that goes back for centuries. A version of it was published in 1549 called "A most strange weddinge of the ffrogge and the mowse." By 1770 or so, this little ballad was understood to be for children. It's the kind of song that answers its own questions, except at the end, when it seems to get bored, and suddenly starts speaking directly to a reader or listener who's been following all along.

A frog went walking one fine day,
    A-hmmm, A-hmmm,
A frog went walking one fine day,
He met Miss Mousie on the way.
    A-hmmm, A-hmmm.

He said, "Miss Mousie will you marry me?"
    A-hmmm, A-hmmm,
He said, "Miss Mousie will you marry me?"
We'll live together in a hollow tree.
    A-hmmm, A-hmmm.

The first to the wedding was farmer Brown,
    A-hmmm, A-hmmm,
The first to the wedding was farmer Brown,
He brought his wife in a wedding-gown.
    A-hmmm, A-hmmm.

The second to the wedding was Doctor Dick,
    A-hmmm, A-hmmm,
The second to the wedding was Doctor Dick,
He ate so much that he nearly got sick.
    A-hmmm, A-hmmm.

20

The third to the wedding was Grandma Green,
A-hmmm, A-hmmm,
The third to the wedding was Grandma Green,
Her shawl was blue but it wasn't clean.
A-hmmm, A-hmmm.

And what do you think they had for supper?
A-hmmm, A-hmmm,
And what do you think they had for supper?
Some fried mosquitoes without any butter.
A-hmmm, A-hmmm.

And what do you think they had for a fiddle?
A-hmmm, A-hmmm,
And what do you think they had for a fiddle?
An old tin can with a hole in the middle.
A-hmmm, A-hmmm.

And what do you think they had on the shelf?
A-hmmm, A-hmmm,
And what do you think they had on the shelf?
If you want to find out, go look for yourself!
A-hmmm, A-hmmm.

THE MAN-OF-WAR HAWK

Herman Melville (1819–1891)

The man-of-war bird is usually known by the name of frigate bird; it has long, powerful wings and dark plumage, and flies over the ocean. The great American novelist Herman Melville, author of Moby Dick, sailed on whaling boats when he was young. Melville was also a remarkable poet. Even in these few lines, his description is very energetic: the dark bird in the light of the sky flies above the dark ship with its sail that's like a cloud lit by the sun. In reading this poem aloud, you'll notice that the rhythm of the lines—roughly da dum da da dum da da dum da da dum—is hard to sound out at the beginning, but in the last two lines, the rhythm is as strong and clear as the flight of the bird itself.

Yon black man-of-war hawk that wheels in the light
O'er the black ship's white sky-s'l, sunned cloud to the sight,
Have we low-flyers wings to ascend to his height?

No arrow can reach him; nor thought can attain
To the placid supreme in the sweep of his reign.

sky-s'l—*sky-sail (spelled here the way it's*
   pronounced): the highest, smallest sail on
   a square-rigged ship
sunned cloud to the sight—*looking like a cloud in sunlight*
attain to—*reach*
placid—*calm*

22

THE RATS
Georg Trakl (1887–1914)

Georg (pronounced "Gay-org") Trakl was a wonderful Austrian poet who died at age 27. This little poem offers a glimpse of a late autumn night—we learn this from the middle two lines of the last stanza. The ghostly moonlight shines on an ordinary and very natural event—rats running about in search of food. But this scene is somehow mysteriously spooky: are the people all asleep? Or have they abandoned the house and barn? For whatever reason, the sounds of the wind "whimper," as if they were themselves in pain, or in fear.

In the yard the autumn moon shines white,
The roof-edge drops fantastic shadows;
A silence dwells in the empty windows
From which the rats now quietly plunge

And flit about, squeaking, here and there;
A grayish misty exhalation
From the outhouse sniffs after them,
Spectral moonlight trembling through it.

And the rats brawl avidly as if mad
Filling up the house and barn-loft
Already full of grain and fruit.
Icy winds whimper in the yard.

exhalation—*breath*
outhouse—*small shack containing a toilet, when
    there is no indoor plumbing*
spectral—*ghostly*

23

EARTHY ANECDOTE

Wallace Stevens (1879–1955)

Anecdotes are very short stories, told aloud or written down, sometimes about a famous person or event, and most often humorous. The great twentieth-century American poet Wallace Stevens called this little account of animals on a plain an "anecdote." But it's a sort of fable about one kind of energy controlling and bringing order to another kind. The bucks "clatter" over Oklahoma until the firecat "bristles"—like a puma or even somehow like a small prairie fire—and turns them to the left and right. It is like herding sheep, or directing traffic—unruly motion is given direction. Finally, the fire-cat itself can leap to the right and left, and, its work for the day done, sleep.

Every time the bucks went clattering
Over Oklahoma
A firecat bristled in the way.

Wherever they went,
They went clattering,
Until they swerved
In a swift, circular line
To the right,
Because of the firecat.

Or until they swerved
In a swift, circular line
To the left,
Because of the firecat.

The bucks clattered.
The firecat went leaping,
To the right, to the left,
And
Bristled in the way.

Later, the firecat closed his bright eyes
And slept.

bucks—*adult, male deer*
firecat—*a mythical animal, apparently*
  something like a mountain lion

HOW DOTH THE LITTLE CROCODILE

Lewis Carroll (1832–1898)

In Lewis Carroll's celebrated Alice in Wonderland, *Alice is often asked by elders to recite a poem from memory (to "speak a piece," it used to be called.) At one point in the story, she is asked to speak "How doth the little—," a very goody-goody moral lesson in verse by the Reverend Isaac Watts, a famous preacher and writer of hymns. Watts' poem is called "Against Idleness and Mischief." It begins:*

*How doth the little busy bee
   Improve each shining hour,
And gather honey all the day
   From every opening flower!*

*How skillfully she builds her cell!
   How neat she spreads the wax!
And labours hard to store it well
   With the sweet food she makes. . .*

As with other recitations Alice manages to come up with, the lines come out delightfully and naughtily wrong.

How doth the little crocodile
   Improve his shining tail,
And pour the waters of the Nile
   On every golden scale!

How cheerfully he seems to grin,
   How neatly spreads his claws,
And welcomes little fishes in,
   With gently smiling jaws!

improve—*make good use of*

26

LITTLE FISH

D. H. Lawrence (1885—1930)

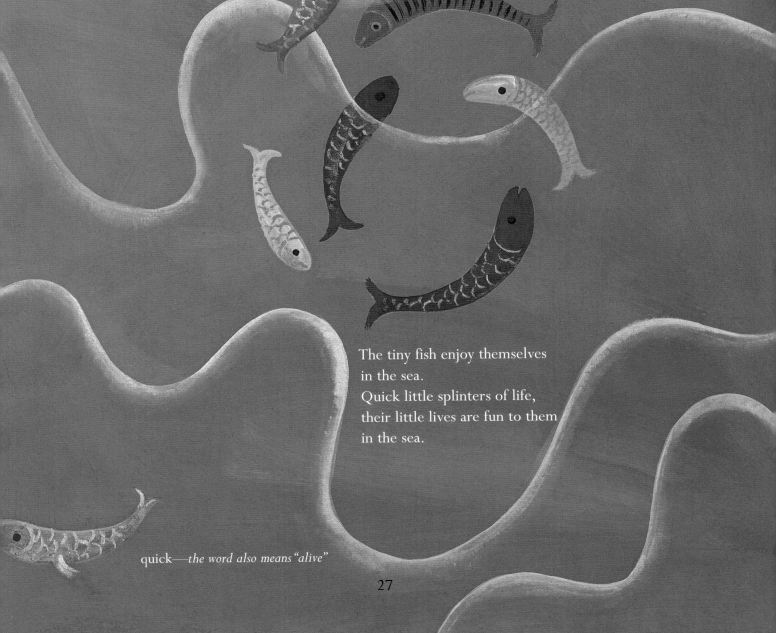

D[avid] H[erbert] Lawrence, a great English novelist of the earlier twentieth century, was a remarkable poet as well. This little observation about very small fish in the vastness of the sea comes from his book called Pansies; *the name of that flower comes from the French word "pensées," meaning "thoughts." Many of the short poems in that book are, like this one, momentary single thoughts. Another, longer poem might go on to thoughts about the fish—about how there are always larger fish to swallow them up. But for this moment, the poet thinks only of their energy, of their rapid motion. It is as if they were points of moving light in a great darkness.*

The tiny fish enjoy themselves
in the sea.
Quick little splinters of life,
their little lives are fun to them
in the sea.

quick—*the word also means "alive"*

27

TO THE GRASSHOPPER AND THE CRICKET

Leigh Hunt (1784–1859)

The great poet John Keats and his friend Leigh Hunt challenged each other to write a sonnet in 15 minutes one day in December of 1816 (Keats was 21, Hunt 11 years older.) They chose as their subject the grasshopper, heard outdoors and in summer, and the cricket usually heard in the house by the warm hearth or fireplace. Both finished their poems in time. Each sonnet is of a different sort, with the rhymes arranged in different patterns. Hunt hears in the songs of both "cousins" a general "Mirth." Keats hears a deeper music of "the poetry of earth."

Green little vaulter in the sunny grass,
   Catching your heart up at the feel of June,
   Sole voice that's heard amidst the lazy noon,
When ev'n the bees lag at the summoning brass;—

And you, warm little housekeeper, who class
   With those who think the candles come too soon,
   Loving the fire, and with your tricksome tune
Nick the glad silent moments as they pass;—

Oh sweet and tiny cousins, that belong,
   One to the fields, the other to the hearth,
Both have your sunshine; both, though small, are strong
   At your clear hearts; and both were sent on earth
To sing in thoughtful ears this natural song—
   In doors and out,—summer and winter,—Mirth.

vaulter—*jumper*
summoning—*calling up*
tricksome—*tricky*
Mirth—*gladness*

ON THE GRASSHOPPER AND CRICKET

John Keats (1795–1821)

The poetry of earth is never dead:
    When all the birds are faint with the hot sun,
    And hide in cooling trees, a voice will run
From hedge to hedge about the new-mown mead;
That is the Grasshopper's—he takes the lead
    In summer luxury,—he has never done
    With his delights; for when tired out with fun
He rests at ease beneath some pleasant weed.
The poetry of earth is ceasing never:
    On a lone winter evening, when the frost
    Has wrought a silence, from the stove there shrills
The Cricket's song, in warmth increasing ever,
    And seems to one in drowsiness half lost,
    The Grasshopper's among some grassy hills.

mead—*field*
has never done—*is never finished*
one—*anyone*

29

THE EAGLE

Alfred, Lord Tennyson (1809–1892)

Lord Tennyson was one of the two greatest English poets of the nineteenth century. Many of his works are quite long. But this very short piece he called a "fragment"—as if it had been broken off from a longer poem—is strong, almost like the eagle itself, and very memorable. It pictures something very ordinary and natural: eagles frequently go fishing for their food, as gulls and other seabirds do. But there's nothing ordinary in the language describing the scene. Rather, there's something almost fairytale-like in "lonely lands," and in seeing the bird on a high peak surrounded by a whole world of sky. On a windy day, from the eagle's great height, the sea would look "wrinkled" by waves, but it "crawls" almost as if it, too, were some slow animal.

He clasps the crag with crooked hands;
Close to the sun in lonely lands,
Ringed with the azure world, he stands.

The wrinkled sea beneath him crawls;
He watches from his mountain walls.
And like a thunderbolt he falls.

crag——*rock jutting out of a cliff*
azure——*sky-blue*

30

CLOCK-A-CLAY

John Clare (1793–1864)

John Clare came from a family of farm workers, and wrote about nature in a very original way. He struggled with insanity most of his life, but his poems remained clear and strong. In this one, the speaker, lying among wildflowers, thinks of himself as a ladybug; by the third stanza, it is the bug itself who speaks, as if the poet had actually become the ladybug. He also thinks of it in connection with ordinary clocks, watches, and keeping time generally.

In the cowslip pips I lie,
Hidden from a buzzing fly,
While green grass beneath me lies,
Pearled with dew like fishes' eyes,
Here I lie, a clock-a-clay,
Waiting for the time of day.

While grassy forest quakes surprise,
And the wild wind sobs and sighs,
My gold home rocks as like to fall,
On its pillar green and tall;
While the pattering rain drives by
Clock-a-clay keeps warm and dry.

Day by day and night by night,
All the week I hide from sight;
In the cowslip pips I lie,
In rain and dew still warm and dry;
Day and night, and night and day,
Red, black-spotted clock-a-clay.

My home shakes in wind and showers,
Pale green pillar topped with flowers,
Bending at the wild wind's breath,
Till I touch the grass beneath;
Here I live, lone clock-a-clay,
Watching for the time of day.

Clock-a-clay—*the ladybug or ladybird. In Clare's part of England, beetles are called "clocks."*
cowslip pips—*blossoms of a kind of yellow primrose flower, common in England*
quakes surprise—*shakes with surprise*
as like to—*as if it were to*

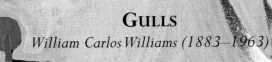

GULLS
William Carlos Williams (1883–1963)

Williams was a doctor who lived and practiced in Rutherford, New Jersey, while writing some of the finest American poetry of the twentieth century. This is a sort of fable in which the gulls stand for interesting people and new experiences and imagination beyond the lives of the townspeople addressed by the speaker. But the beauty and calmness of the flight of these birds leave the speaker without anger or hostility towards the townspeople he finds so limiting.

My townspeople, beyond in the great world,
are many with whom it were far more
profitable for me to live than here with you.
These whirr about me calling, calling!
and for my own part I answer them, loud as I can,
but they, being free, pass!
I remain! Therefore, listen!
For you will not soon have another singer.

First I say this: You have seen
the strange birds, have you not, that sometimes
rest upon our river in winter?
Let them cause you to think well then of the storms
that drive many to shelter. These things
do not happen without reason.

And the next thing I say is this:
I saw an eagle once circling against the clouds
over one of our principal churches—
Easter, it was—a beautiful day!
three gulls came from above the river
and crossed slowly seaward!
Oh, I know you have your own hymns, I have heard them—
and because I knew they invoked some great protector
I could not be angry with you, no matter
how much they outraged true music—

You see, it is not necessary for us to leap at each other,
and, as I told you, in the end
the gulls moved seaward very quietly.

invoked—*called up*
outraged—*offended imaginativeness*

33

BISON CROSSING NEAR MT. RUSHMORE

May Swenson (1919–1989)

The National Monument of Mt. Rushmore, in the Black Hills of South Dakota, has 60-foot-high images of Presidents Washington, Jefferson, Lincoln and Theodore Roosevelt carved into it. But a poet can see a herd of bison as a kind of national treasure as well. They are a "somber remnant of western freedom" at a time when this American buffalo had become almost extinct. May Swenson, one of the finest and most original poets of her time, came from Utah, but wrote her poems in and near New York. In this poem she sees the tourists coming to Mt. Rushmore as something like a herd of animals, less interesting than the very closely observed bison.

There is our herd of cars stopped,
staring respectfully at the line of bison crossing.
One big-fronted bull nudges his cow into a run.
She and her calf are first to cross.
In swift dignity the dark-coated caravan sweeps through
the gap our cars leave in the two-way stall
on the road to the Presidents.
The polygamous bulls guarding their families from the rear,
the honey-brown calves trotting head-to-hip
by their mothers—who are lean and muscled as bulls,
with chin tassels and curved horns—
all leap the road like a river, and run.
The strong and somber remnant of western freedom
disappears into the rough grass of the draw,
around the point of the mountain.
The bison, orderly, disciplined by the prophet-faced,
heavy-headed fathers, threading the pass
of our awestruck stationwagons, airstreams and trailers,
if in dread of us give no sign,
go where their leaders twine them, over the prairie.
And we keep to our line,
staring, stirring, revving idling motors, moving
each behind the other, herdlike, where the highway leads.

caravan—*single file of vehicles*
polygamous—*having many wives*
somber—*dark and gloomy*
draw—*wide ditch*
airstreams—*streamlined cars*
revving—*running a car engine with the clutch in or the gears in neutral*

THE CAT AND THE MOON
William Butler Yeats (1865–1939)

Yeats was one of the greatest poets of the early twentieth century, who lived in his native Ireland and often used its folk-lore and mythology in his poems. Minnaloushe was the name of a cat belonging to the poet's friend Maud Gonne. At the beginning of this poem Yeats calls the cat "the nearest kin of the moon." This is because the moon undergoes changes through its phases during any month, and the pupils of a cat's eye change, in different degrees of light, from narrowed slits to fully round. The thought of an actual cat, dancing in the moonlight, leads the poet to imagine a strange and mysterious relationship between the cat and the moon that is "sacred" to it.

The cat went here and there
And the moon spun round like a top,
And the nearest kin of the moon,
The creeping cat, looked up.
Black Minnaloushe stared at the moon,
For, wander and wail as he would,
The pure cold light in the sky
Troubled his animal blood.
Minnaloushe runs in the grass
Lifting his delicate feet.
Do you dance, Minnaloushe, do you dance?
When two close kindred meet,
What better than call a dance?
Maybe the moon may learn,
Tired of that courtly fashion,
A new dance turn.
Minnaloushe creeps through the grass
From moonlit place to place,
The sacred moon overhead
Has taken a new phase.
Does Minnaloushe know that his pupils
Will pass from change to change,
And that from round to crescent,
From crescent to round they range?
Minnaloushe creeps through the grass
Alone, important and wise,
And lifts to the changing moon
His changing eyes.

that courtly fashion—*the moon's grave, slow rate of change*
kindred—*relatives*

37

THE CROW AND THE FOX
Jean de La Fontaine (1621–1695)

The most famous writer of many animal fables in verse (Aesop's were in prose) was Jean de La Fontaine, a French poet who often wrote in the later seventeenth century. School children in France, and elsewhere in French classes at school, all know this tale. It concerns a crafty fox (we use the term "foxy" to talk of clever, scheming people) and a crow who is more vain than he is smart. La Fontaine worked out a lively poetic form for his fables, moving back and forth from long lines to short ones.

Mister Crow, perched high in a tree,
    Held a cheese in his beak;
    Mister Fox liked its smell, and he
Called up to him in these words (so to speak)
    "Hello there, Mr. Crow!
    How fine you look, how handsome! Should
    Your singing be like your plumage, well,
    Then, truth to tell,

You'd be the grandest bird in all the wood!
    At these words, Crow starts to rejoice
    And then to show off his gorgeous voice
Opens his large beak and drops the cheese.
    Fox grabs it, and says "Good Sir,
    Learn that all flatterers depend
On some dope who's an eager listener.
This lesson's worth a cheese, at least, in the end."
    Ashamed, confused, Crow swore—too late—
    He'd not again end up in such a state.

flatterers—*people who pay exaggerated and insincere compliments*

RIDING A NERVOUS HORSE

Vicki Hearne (1946–2001)

Vicki Hearne, born in Texas, lived in California and Connecticut, and was a trainer of horses and dogs who wrote both fine poetry and philosophical essays on relations between people and animals. Here she distinguishes between merely admiring the beauty of the horse by observers (she calls them "horse eaters") and the attention that the poet must pay to the horse's feelings and character while riding him.

A dozen false starts:
You're such a fool, I said,
Spooking at shadows when
All day you were calm,
Placidly nosing the bushes
That now you pretend are
     strange,
Are struck with menace.

But he shuddered, stubborn
In his horsy posture,
Saying that I brought
Devils with me that he
Could hear gathering in all
The places behind him as I
Diverted his coherence
With my chatter and tack.

Indeed I have stolen
Something, a careful attention
I claim for my own yearning
Purpose, while he
Is left alone to guard
Us both from horse eaters
That merely grin at me
But lust for him, for
The beauty of the haunch
My brush has polished, revealing
Treasures of edible light
In the shift of hide and hooves.

coherence—*the way all the parts of his body worked together; coordination*
tack—*saddle, bridle, riding boots, etc.*
horse eaters—*the poet doesn't mean literally eating horses, but admiring them*
    possessively, the way they find the light reflected from his body "edible"
brush—*used to brush his coat*

A Noiseless, Patient Spider
Walt Whitman (1819–1892)

The great American nineteenth-century poet Walt Whitman considers a spider's web in these lines. He observes the delicacy and immense strength of the frail threads of the web. Then he thinks of his own desire to "connect," through his poems and his feelings, something inside himself with all that lies beyond him.

A noiseless patient spider,
I mark'd where on a little promontory it stood isolated,
Mark'd how to explore the vacant vast surrounding,
It launch'd forth filament, filament, filament, out of itself,
Ever unreeling them, ever tirelessly speeding them.

And you O my Soul where you stand,
Surrounded, detached, in measureless oceans of space,
Ceaselessly musing, venturing, throwing, seeking the spheres to connect them,
Till the bridge you will need be form'd, till the ductile anchor hold,
Till the gossamer thread you fling catch somewhere, O my Soul

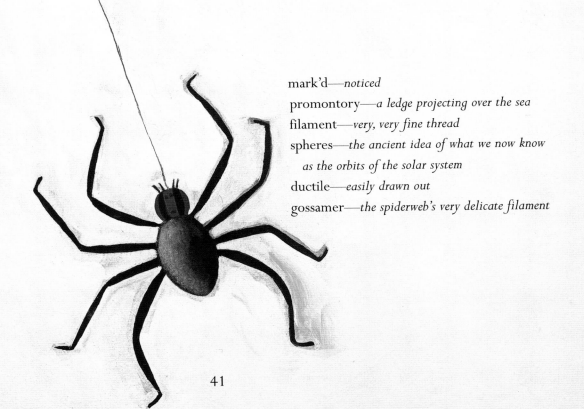

mark'd—*noticed*
promontory—*a ledge projecting over the sea*
filament—*very, very fine thread*
spheres—*the ancient idea of what we now know
    as the orbits of the solar system*
ductile—*easily drawn out*
gossamer—*the spiderweb's very delicate filament*

FROG AND TOAD
Christina Rossetti (1830–1894)

Christina Rossetti was a Victorian poet, like her brother Dante Gabriel Rossetti who was also a painter. Both of these little poems deal with people's obligations to animals ("the dumb"—animals used to be referred to as "the dumb beasts" because they couldn't speak). The speaker of the first poem could be either a child or a good-humored adult. The speaker of the second echoes the language and spirit of Proverbs or Ecclesiastes in the Bible.

Hopping frog, hop here and be seen,
   I'll not pelt you with stick or stone:
Your cap is laced and your coat is green;
   Good bye, we'll let each other alone.

Plodding toad, plod here and be looked at,
You the finger of scorn is crooked at:
But though you're lumpish, you're harmless too;
You won't hurt me, and I won't hurt you.

pelt—*throw at*
plod—*move heavily*
scorn—*contempt*

A WORD FOR THE DUMB

Pity the sorrows of a poor old Dog
   Who wags his tail a-begging in his need:
Despise not even the sorrows of a Frog,
   God's creature too, and that's enough to plead:
Spare Puss who trusts us purring on our hearth:
   Spare Bunny once so frisky and so free:
Spare all the harmless tenants of the earth:
   Spare, and be spared:—or who shall plead for thee?

despise—*hate*
hearth—*fireplace*
thee—*you*

42

TO A BUTTERFLY

William Wordsworth (1770–1850)

William Wordsworth was one of the very greatest English poets who wrote and thought about nature and our knowledge of it. Here, he addresses a butterfly, taking delight in watching it alight among flowers planted by his beloved sister, Dorothy (whom he calls "Emmeline" later in the poem.) The second stanza ends with a momentary thought of his youth. This leads to thinking of the butterfly, in the rest of the poem, as a "historian of our infancy." It is a living souvenir of their childhood, and of Dorothy's gentle and loving character. And it also reminds us that a butterfly's wings are as fragile as they are beautiful.

I've watched you now a full half-hour;
Self-poised upon that yellow flower
And, little Butterfly! indeed
I know not if you sleep or feed.
How motionless!—not frozen seas
More motionless! and then
What joy awaits you, when the breeze
Hath found you out among the trees,
And calls you forth again!

This plot of orchard-ground is ours;
My trees they are, my Sister's flowers;
Here rest your wings when they are weary;
Here lodge as in a sanctuary!
Come often to us, fear no wrong;
Sit near us on the bough!
We'll talk of sunshine and of song,
And summer days, when we were young;
Sweet childish days, that were as long
As twenty days are now.

Stay near me—do not take thy flight!
A little longer stay in sight!
Much converse do I find in thee,
Historian of my infancy!
Float near me; do not yet depart!
Dead times revive in thee:
Thou bring'st, gay creature as thou art!
A solemn image to my heart,
My father's family!

Oh! pleasant, pleasant were the days,
The time, when, in our childish plays,
My sister Emmeline and I
Together chased the butterfly!
A very hunter did I rush
Upon the prey:—with leaps and springs
I followed on from brake to bush;
But she, God love her, feared to brush
The dust from off its wings.

sanctuary—*safe place of refuge*
brake—*thicket, undergrowth*
converse—*talk of thoughts and feelings*

Hunting Song of the Seeonee Pack

Rudyard Kipling (1865–1936)

Kipling lived in India for the earlier part of his life, and wrote wonderfully of it both in prose and rhyme. This is from a story about a pack of wolves [the "Seeonee pack"] and a human boy named Mowgli whom they protect and educate. Wolves live and hunt together in very organized ways. Kipling imagines these words as being sung by some of the wolves in his story.

As the dawn was breaking the Sambhur belled—
    Once, twice and again!
And a doe leaped up, and a doe leaped up
From the pond in the wood where the wild deer sup.
This I, scouting alone, beheld,
    Once, twice and again!

As the dawn was breaking the Sambhur belled—
    Once, twice and again!
And a wolf stole back, and a wolf stole back
To carry the word to the waiting pack,
And we sought and we found and we bayed on his track
    Once, twice and again!

As the dawn was breaking the Wolf-Pack yelled
    Once, twice and again!
Feet in the jungle that leave no mark!
Eyes that can see in the dark—the dark!
Tongue—give tongue to it! Hark! O hark!
    Once, twice and again!

Sambhur—*a kind of Asian deer [pronounced to rhyme with amber]*
belled—*bellowed, cried out*
bayed—*howled*
give tongue to it!—*speak up!*

TO A SQUIRREL AT
KYLE-NA-NO

William Butler Yeats
(1865–1939)

*Kyle-na-no was one of the woods on
the grounds of Coole Park, an estate
in northern Ireland belonging to
Yeats' friend, Lady Gregory. In Irish
its name means "Wood of nuts,"
certainly an appropriate place for a
squirrel to be. The squirrel in these
lines seems to be behaving in the
familiar way squirrels have—sitting
watching you and then very
suddenly darting quickly away.*

Come play with me;
Why should you run
Through the shaking tree
As though I'd a gun
To strike you dead?
When all I would do
Is to scratch your head
And let you go.

THE CREATURES REST

Alcman (seventh century B.C.E.)

Alcman was a very ancient Greek poet who lived in the seventh century B.C.E. Like the work of the great poet Sappho (who lived around 50 years later), only fragments of his poems survive. These beautiful lines make up a well-shaped poem in themselves. The reason we still have them is that a Greek scholar who lived many centuries later quoted them in a discussion of animals. In poetry composed of lists of things, the order in which we hear of them is very important. Here, we start with the mountaintops—the earth itself—in "sleep" and end up with the birds, bringing the poem back to the heights from which it started. Calling the birds "wide-winged" is very typical of Greek poetry; it also means that the birds fly far and wide over sea and land.

Now sleep mountain-top and chasm
headland and ravine,
creeping kinds that emerge from the black earth
beasts who roam the hillside, the race of bees,
and creatures submerged in the purple sea
now sleep, and tribes,
too, of the wide-winged.

chasms—*deep cracks in the ground*
headlands—*high points of land that extend, with a sheer drop, into a body of water*
ravines—*chasms worn down by flowing water*

47

INDEX